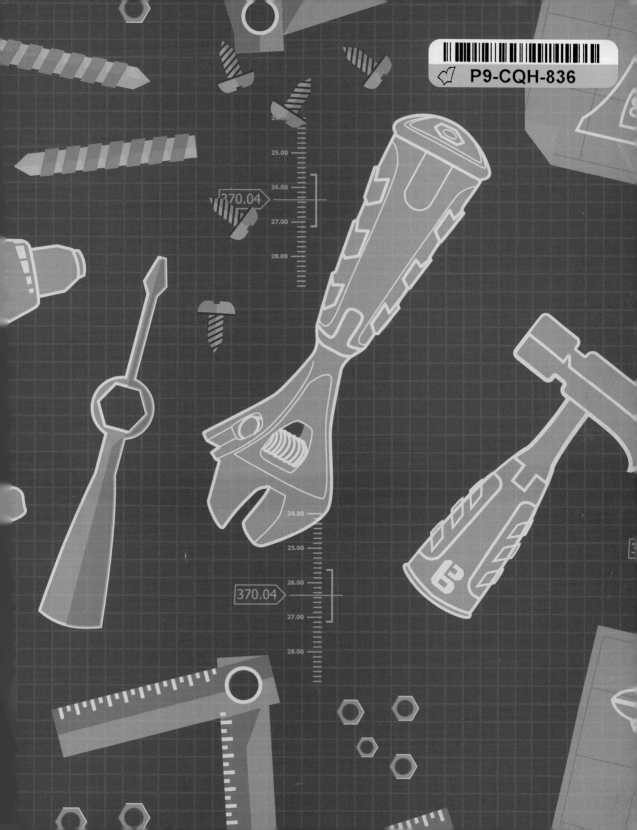

370.04

370.04

This edition published by Parragon Books Ltd in 2016

Parragon Books Ltd
Chartist House
15–17 Trim Street
Bath BA1 1HA, UK
www.parragon.com

ISBN 978-1-4748-4711-7

Printed in China

Bath • New York • Cologne • Melbourne • Delhi
Hong Kong • Shenzhen • Singapore

Bob and Wendy are constructing a new penguin pool at Spring City Zoo. Lofty is there to help – he can lift the huge blocks of ice into the pool.

"I think the penguins are really going to enjoy their new home," says Bob.

"What penguins?" asks Lofty.

Wendy smiles. "They'll be here soon," she says. "Don't worry."

Two-Tonne, the heavy-lifting lorry, is bringing the penguins to the zoo. Bob, Wendy and Lofty need to finish the pool before Two-Tonne arrives. The penguins will need to go straight into the water when they get here.

Meanwhile, Leo is working at the Town Hall. With the help of Scoop, he has finished building a new fountain in the garden. Leo turns on the water.

"Well done, Leo," says Scoop. "It's great!"

Mayor Madison is also at the Town Hall, talking to Mr Bentley about a special visitor that will be arriving soon – Mayor Snipe from Riverdale.

"Mayor Snipe can be difficult to please," says Mayor Madison. "We must make sure he enjoys his visit."

"Don't worry," Mr Bentley replies. "We are going to show Mayor Snipe all the best places in Spring City!"

Back at the zoo, the new penguin pool is almost finished. Lofty is lifting one last ice block, but he is so excited that he drives too fast and drops the ice block against the glass wall of the pool.

"Oh no!" cries Lofty, "I'm sorry, Bob, I was just so excited about seeing the penguins!"

Bob inspects the glass.

"Hmm," he says, "there's a nasty crack."

"We can't fill the pool with water until we get that fixed," says Wendy.

"It'll need a new window," Bob decides. "I just hope we have time before the penguins arrive."

But, at that very moment, Two-Tonne arrives with the penguins!
"I'm afraid the pool isn't quite ready," Bob tells Two-Tonne.
Everyone is worried. The penguins shouldn't stay inside their
travel crate for much longer. They need room to waddle around
and somewhere to swim.

Just then, Lofty has an idea. "The penguins can go to the new fountain at the Town Hall until the glass wall is replaced," he says.

Leo has just arrived at the zoo with Scoop.

"Oh yes, it's perfect," says Leo. He tells the others that Mayor Madison is going to be out all day with her visitor. She won't even know the penguins have been there.

Leo, Scoop and Two-Tonne take the penguins to the Town Hall, while the others stay at the zoo to fix the glass window.

"Let's get the penguins out of that crate," says Leo.

"They're not going to fly away are they?" asks Scoop.

"Oh no," says Two-Tonne, "they haven't got wings. Those are flippers. They can swim but they can't fly."

The penguins love being in the water after their journey.

On the other side of town, Mayor Madison
and Mr Bentley are showing Mayor Snipe around
Fixham Castle. It is the oldest monument in
Spring City.

But Mayor Snipe isn't impressed – he doesn't
like old buildings.

Next, they try showing Mayor Snipe a fantastic new
building in the city – the magnificent sports stadium.
    But Mayor Snipe still isn't impressed.
    "I'm not very keen on sports," he says. "Not my thing."
    Mayor Madison and Mr Bentley are getting worried.
Is Mayor Snipe going to like anything about Spring City?

At the zoo, Muck has arrived to help.
"Here's the new window, Bob!" Muck says.
"Excellent!" says Bob. "Okay, everyone,
we need to get those penguins into
their new pool as soon as possible.
Can we fix it?"
"Yes, we can!" everybody
answers, and they get
straight to work.

Meanwhile, at the Town Hall fountain,
Leo and Scoop are finding it difficult
to keep the penguins under control.
The birds are waddling all over the place!
"Get back here!" Leo cries.

"It's lucky Mayor Madison isn't around to see this," says Scoop.
"It's okay, Scoop," says Leo, "she won't be back for hours!"

Mayor Madison and Mr Bentley have decided to
take their visitor to a wonderful revolving restaurant.
    But, of course, Mayor Snipe doesn't like it.
    "I feel sick!" he cries.
    When Mayor Snipe runs off towards the bathroom,
Mayor Madison puts her head in her hands.
    "This visit has been a complete disaster!" she cries.

After that, Mayor Madison and Mr Bentley take Mayor Snipe straight back to the Town Hall.

When they arrive, Leo and Scoop are still chasing around after the penguins!

"Who is responsible for this?" asks Mayor Madison in a panic.

But Mayor Snipe has a huge smile on his face.

"Penguins!" he cries. "How did you know that I love penguins?"

Mayor Madison can't believe it – her visitor is finally happy!

Just then, Bob arrives from
the zoo to collect the penguins.
He sees Mayor Madison and
worries she will be angry.

"Hi Bob!" says Leo, before
anyone else can speak.
"Turns out the special guest
really likes penguins!"

Bob quickly thinks of
a great idea. "And that's why
Mayor Madison has arranged
for you to come back to
the zoo," he tells Mayor Snipe,
"and officially open our new
penguin pool!"

"Oh, I'd love that!"
says the happy visitor.

Everybody heads to the zoo for the grand opening of the new penguin pool.

Mayor Snipe loves being the one to let the penguins out of their crate and into their new home.

"I now declare Spring City's new Antarctic Penguin Experience well and truly open!" he announces.

The penguin pool is fantastic. Everybody stands by the new glass window and watches the penguins swimming around under the water.

Mayor Snipe is very happy. "This has been the best visit ever," he says. "Thank you, Mayor Madison and thank you, Mr Bentley."

"And thank you, Bob," Mayor Madison says quietly, so Mayor Snipe doesn't hear. "Once again, you have saved the day."